WHERE ARE THE COOKIES?

Sonia B. F. Arias

ISBN: 9798829410810

escritoreslattnoamericanos @gmaiil.com

To my dear Sebastian with all my love from Great grandma.
I hope you like it.

Let me tell you the story of a cookie jar that was at my grandma's house.

When I saw it the first time, it was full of cookies.

But the following day, I went to grab a cookie and guess what?

The cookies were all gone! The jar was empty!

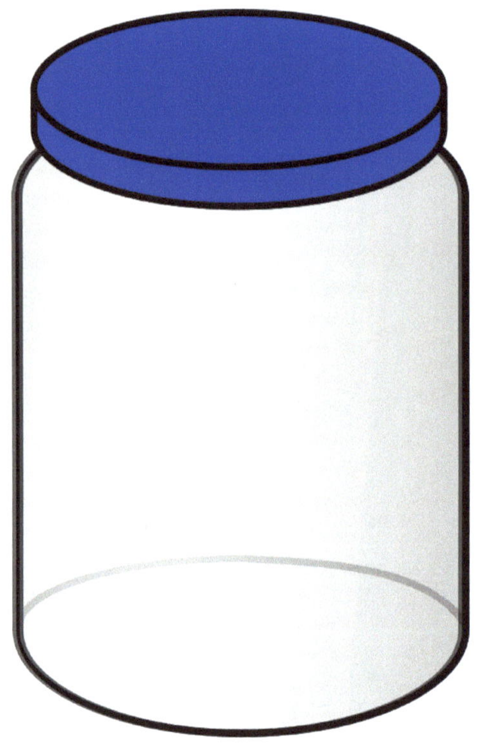

I asked grandma and she didn't know what happened.

My papa said: "I think it was your cousins, because they came to visit last night."

I was sad, really sad, because I was not here when they came. I was at my dad's house.

But my grandpa made me laugh, telling me some good riddles about cookies.

My grandpa likes riddles. Sometimes, they
are hard to guess, but I'm smart and most of
the time I know the answer.

One of my cousins can not guess the riddles. He says he is not good at guessing.

My dad says he is not good at riddles either, but he is good at playing basketball.

My papa likes cookies. He bakes cookies with me. He is the one that bakes cookies at my grandma's house.

My dog Fido likes cookies, but grandma says dogs get sick if they eat them.

My auntie is coming next Friday. I am excited. She told me she will bring me a big box of cookies.

I guess that if dogs can not eat cookies, cats can not eat them either.

My uncle Chris is a dentist, and he says cookies are not good for my teeth.

My aunt Emily is a nurse, and she says that, if I eat cookies only once a week, I'll be fine.

This is a picture of me and my friends at school. We all like cookies!
Yummy, yummy for my tummy!

Let me tell you a secret. Tomorrow is my teacher's birthday, and I am bringing some chocolate chip cookies for her and the class.

The end

Printed in USA
California
Mundo Latino Publications
escritoreslatinoamericanos@gmail.com